BEATRIX POTTER ™
BEDTIME STORIES

BEATRIX POTTER ™
BEDTIME STORIES

From The World of Peter Rabbit and Friends ™

F. WARNE & Co

This edition published exclusively for Dealerfield Ltd by
FREDERICK WARNE

Published by the Penguin Group
27 Wrights Lane, London W8 5TZ, England
Penguin Books USA Inc., 375 Hudson Street, New York, New York 10014, USA
Penguin Books Australia Ltd, Ringwood, Victoria, Australia
Penguin Books Canada Ltd, 10 Alcorn Avenue, Toronto, Ontario, Canada M4V 3B2
Penguin Books (N.Z.) Ltd, 182-190 Wairau Road, Auckland 10, New Zealand

Penguin Books Ltd, Registered Offices: Harmondsworth, Middlesex, England

This edition first published by Frederick Warne & Co. 1996
1 3 5 7 9 10 8 6 4 2

ISBN 0 7232 4385 9

Manufactured in China by Imago Publishing Limited

CONTENTS

THE TALE OF
PETER RABBIT
AND
BENJAMIN BUNNY

Once upon a time there were four little rabbits, and their names were
Flopsy, Mopsy, Cotton-tail and Peter.

They lived with their mother in a sandbank, underneath the root of a
very big fir-tree.

'Now, then,' said Mrs Rabbit one morning to her children, 'you may go
into the fields, or down the lane but don't go into Mr McGregor's garden.
Your father had an accident there - he was put in a pie by Mrs McGregor.'

'Run along now and don't get into mischief. I'm going out,' said Mrs Rabbit.

Then she took her basket and umbrella and went through the wood to the baker.

Flopsy, Mopsy and Cotton-tail, who were good little bunnies, went down the lane to gather blackberries.

But Peter, who was very naughty, ran off towards Mr McGregor's garden. On the way he saw his cousin Benjamin.

'Meet me tomorrow - at the big fir tree!' Benjamin whispered.

Peter squeezed under the gate into Mr McGregor's garden.

'Mama will never find out,' he said to himself.

First he ate some lettuces and some French beans; and then he ate some radishes.

'Ooh! My favourite,' he said happily, 'I can't wait to tell Benjamin.'

Peter ate so many radishes that he began to feel rather sick.

'Oh,' he groaned, 'I had better find a little bit of parsley,' and off he went to search for some.

But whom do you think he should meet round the end of a cucumber frame?

'Oh help!' gasped Peter. 'It's Mr McGregor!'

Mr McGregor was planting out young cabbages, but he jumped up and was after Peter in no time, shouting, 'Stop, thief!'

Peter was most dreadfully frightened; he rushed all over the garden, for he had forgotten the way back to the gate. He lost his shoes and ran faster on all fours. Indeed, Peter might have got away altogether if he had not run into a gooseberry net.

'Hurry, Peter, hurry,' urged some friendly sparrows.
'Mr McGregor's coming! Quick, you must keep trying.'
'It's no use,' sobbed Peter trying to struggle free, 'my brass buttons are all caught up.'

Mr McGregor came up with a sieve, which he intended to pop on the top of Peter, but Peter wriggled free leaving his jacket behind him.

He rushed into the toolshed, and jumped into a watering can. It would have been a beautiful thing to hide in if it had not had so much water in it.

'Come on oot, ye wee beastie -
I know you're here somewhere,'
muttered Mr McGregor,
searching for Peter under the
flower pots.

Suddenly, Peter sneezed,
'Kertyschoo!' and
Mr McGregor was after him in
no time.

Peter jumped out of a window
and ran off.

Peter was quite lost. He found a door in a wall; but it was locked and there was no room for a fat little rabbit to squeeze underneath.

He saw a little old mouse carrying peas to her family.

'If you please, Ma'am, could you tell me the way to the gate?' he asked.

'Mmmm,' was all she could mumble in reply.

'Oh, but which way?' asked Peter sadly, and he began to cry.

Presently, Peter came to a pond where a white cat was staring at some goldfish.

'I must be quiet,' he said to himself. 'Cousin Benjamin has warned me about cats.'

And then Peter saw the gate. He ran as fast as he could, slipped under the gate, and was safe at last in the wood outside the garden.

Mr McGregor hung up the little jacket and the shoes for a scarecrow to frighten the blackbirds.

'Where have you been?' asked Peter's mother. 'And where are your clothes? That is the second little jacket and pair of shoes you've lost in a fortnight. You're to go straight to bed without any supper and I will make you some camomile tea.'

But Flopsy, Mopsy and Cotton-tail had bread and milk and blackberries for supper.

The next day Benjamin Bunny was sitting on a bank waiting for Peter.

'Where has Peter got to?' he wondered, when suddenly he heard the trit trot, trit trot of a pony.

'Well, what luck! It's Mr and Mrs McGregor going out! I'd better find Peter right away,' he thought and rushed off to find his cousin.

Benjamin found Peter sitting alone,
wrapped only in a red cotton
pocket-handkerchief and looking
very sorry for himself.

'I say!' exclaimed Benjamin. 'You
do look poorly. Who has got your
clothes?'

'The scarecrow in Mr McGregor's
garden,' replied Peter and he told
Benjamin what had happened the
day before.

Benjamin laughed. 'That's what I
came to tell you. Mr McGregor has
gone out in the gig, *and* Mrs
McGregor.'

They made their way to
Mr McGregor's garden and got up
onto the wall. They looked down.
Peter's coat and shoes were plainly
to be seen on the scarecrow, topped
with an old tam-o-shanter of
Mr McGregor's.

'It spoils people's clothes to
squeeze under a gate,' said
Benjamin. 'The *proper* way to get in,
is to climb down a pear tree.'

Little Benjamin said that the first
thing to be done was to get back
Peter's clothes.

There had been rain during the
night; there was water in the shoes
and the coat was somewhat shrunk.

'We can use the handkerchief to carry onions as a present for Aunt,' said Benjamin as they gathered the bundle together.

'Come along Peter,' urged Benjamin.

Peter was not enjoying himself.

Benjamin on the contrary was perfectly at home and ate a lettuce leaf.

Peter did not eat anything and said he should like to go home. Then he dropped half the onions!

But as they turned a corner, Peter and Benjamin stopped suddenly.
  'Gracious, what now, Benjamin?' asked Peter.
  This is what those little rabbits saw round the corner!

'Quick, under here,' whispered Benjamin. 'She's coming towards us.'

Perhaps the cat liked the smell of onions - because she sat down on top of the basket.

'Now what do we do?' sobbed Peter miserably.

'She'll have to go in for her supper soon,' said Benjamin hopefully.

But the cat slept on the basket for *five hours*.

Mrs Rabbit was getting anxious.

'Mr Bouncer, have you seen my son, Peter? He's been missing all day.'

'Benjamin has taken himself off too,' replied Benjamin's father. 'Leave it to me, ma'am, I think I know where the young rascals have got to. And if I'm right . . .'

'Father!' shouted Benjamin from beneath the basket.

The cat looked up and saw Mr Bouncer prancing along the top of the wall. Mr Bouncer had no opinion whatever of cats and he kicked her into the greenhouse and locked the door.

Mr Bouncer pulled Benjamin from beneath the basket.

'Benjamin first, I think, then Peter . . . Off home with you now.'

Then Mr Bouncer took the handkerchief of onions, and marched those two naughty rabbits all the way home.

When Peter got home his sisters
rushed to greet him.

  'Well, at least you've found your
jacket and shoes, Peter,' said
Mrs Rabbit, relieved to see her son
home safely.

  'There now my dears,' she added,
'all's well that ends well. But let
that be a lesson to you, Peter.'

The Tale of
Tom Kitten
and
Jemima
Puddle-Duck

Once upon a time there were three little kittens, and their names were Mittens, Tom Kitten and Moppet.

They had dear little coats of their own; and they tumbled about the doorstep and played in the dust.

'I do wish Mrs Twitchit would keep her kittens in order,' quacked Jemima Puddle-duck.

One day their mother - Mrs
Tabitha Twitchit - expected friends
to tea; so she fetched her kittens
indoors, to wash and dress them
before her visitors arrived.

First she scrubbed their faces and
then she brushed their fur.

'Stay where you are, you two,' she
warned and she dressed Mittens
and Moppet in clean pinafores.

Then it was Tom's turn.

'Goodness me, Tom, I had not realised quite how much you have grown. Oh dear, oh dear!' sighed Mrs Tabitha Twitchit. 'We'll just have to make the best of it.'

She sewed the buttons back on again, and Tom was squeezed into his best suit.

'Now, keep your frocks clean, children,' said Mrs Tabitha Twitchit. 'You must walk on your hind legs. Keep away from the dirty ash-pit. And from the pigsty - oh, *and* the Puddle-ducks,' she continued.

Then she let the kittens out into the garden to be out of the way.

'Let's climb up the rockery, and sit on the garden wall,' suggested Moppet eagerly.

Moppet's white tucker fell down into the road. 'Never mind,' she said, 'we can fetch it later. Now, where's Tom?'

'He's still down there,' said Mittens, pointing to the rockery below them.

'Come along, Tom, hurry yourself up,' Mittens called.

Tom was all in pieces when he reached the top of the wall; his hat fell off and the rest of his buttons burst.

While Mittens and Moppet tried to pull him together there was a pit pat paddle-pat! and the three Puddle-ducks came along the road. They stopped and stared up at the kittens. Then they caught sight of the kittens' clothes lying at the bottom of the wall!

'Rather fetching, don't you agree, Jemima?' asked Rebeccah, as she tried on Tom's hat.

Mittens laughed so much that she fell off the wall. Moppet and Tom followed her down.

'Come and help me to dress Tom,' said Moppet to Mr Drake Puddle-duck.

But Mr Drake put Tom's clothes on *himself*.

'It is a very fine morning,' he said and he and Jemima and Rebeccah Puddle-duck set off up the road, keeping step - pit pat, paddle pat!

Then Mrs Tabitha Twitchit came down the garden path and saw her
kittens on the wall with no clothes on.

  'Oh, my goodness,' she gasped, 'just look at you! My friends will arrive
any moment and you are not fit to be seen - I am affronted!

  'Straight to your room and not one sound do I wish to hear,' she ordered.

When Mrs Tabitha Twitchit's friends arrived I am sorry to say she told them that her kittens were in bed with the measles; which was not true.

'Dear, dear. What a shame. The poor souls,' exclaimed Henrietta.

But the kittens were not in bed; *not* in the least.

At the tea-party, strange noises were heard from above. 'You did say they were poorly, didn't you, Tabitha dear?' asked Cousin Ribby curiously.

As for the Puddle-ducks, they went into a pond. The clothes all came off because there were no buttons, and they have been looking for them ever since.

Indeed, Jemima was no better at
finding things than she was at
hiding them. She had often tried to
hide her eggs, but they were always
found and carried off. No-one
believed that Jemima had the
patience to sit on her eggs.
  Poor Jemima became quite
desperate.

'I *will* hatch my own eggs, if I have to make a nest right away from the farm,' she said.

So, one fine spring afternoon, Jemima put on her best bonnet and shawl and set off.

Jemima landed in a clearing in the middle of a wood. She began to waddle about in search of a nesting place, when suddenly she was startled to find an elegantly dressed gentleman reading a newspaper.

'Madam, have you lost your way?' he enquired politely.

'Oh, no,' Jemima explained. 'I am trying to find a convenient, dry nesting place so that I may sit on my eggs.'

54

'Is that so? Indeed! How interesting! As to a nest there is no difficulty: I have a sackful of feathers in my wood-shed,' said the bushy long-tailed gentleman. He opened the door to show Jemima.

 'You will be in nobody's way. You may sit there as long as you like,' he assured her.

'Goodness,' thought Jemima, 'I've never seen so many feathers in one place. Very comfortable, though, and perfect for making my nest, so warm . . . so dry.'

The sandy-whiskered gentleman promised to take great care of Jemima's nest until she came back again the next day.

'Nothing I love better than eggs and ducklings. I should be proud to see a fine nestful in my wood-shed. Oh, what would be a finer sight?'

Jemima Puddle-duck came every afternoon, and laid nine eggs in the nest. The foxy gentleman admired them immensely.

At last Jemima told the gentleman she was ready to sit on her eggs until they hatched.

'Madam,' he said, 'before you commence your tedious sitting I intend to give you a treat. Let us have a dinner party all to ourselves. May I ask you to bring some herbs from the farm garden to make, er . . . a savoury omelette? I will provide lard for the stuffing . . . I mean, omelette.'

Jemima Puddle-duck was a simpleton; she quite unsuspectingly went round nibbling snippets off all the different sorts of herbs that are used for stuffing roast duck.

'What are you doing with those onions?' asked Kep, the collie dog. 'And where do you go every afternoon by yourself?'

Jemima told him the whole story.

'Now, exactly where is your nest?' enquired Kep suspiciously.

Jemima went up the cart-road for the last time and flew over the wood.

When she arrived the bushy long-tailed gentleman was waiting for her.

'Come into the house just as soon as you've looked at your eggs,' he ordered sharply. Jemima had never heard him speak like that. She felt surprised and uncomfortable.

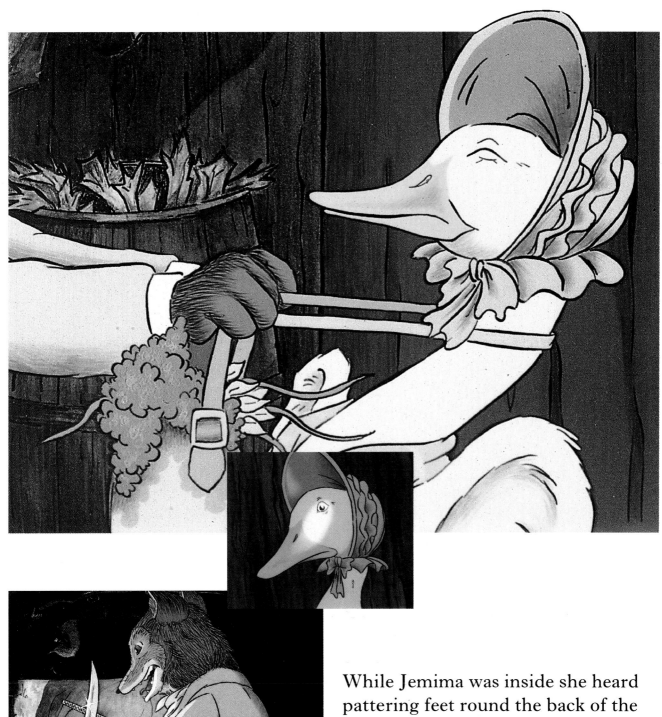

While Jemima was inside she heard
pattering feet round the back of the
shed. She became much alarmed.
  'Oh, what shall I do?' she worried.

A moment afterwards there were the most awful noises - barking, growls and howls, squealing and groans.

'And I think that is the last we will
see of that foxy-whiskered
gentleman,' said Kep.

Unfortunately the puppies had gobbled up all of Jemima's eggs before Kep could stop them.

'There, there, Jemima,' comforted Kep, 'I'm afraid it's just in the nature of things - best make our way home to the farmyard, where you belong, my dear.'

Poor Jemima Puddle-duck was escorted home.

Jemima laid some more eggs in June and she was allowed to keep them herself; but only four of them hatched. She said that it was because of her nerves, but she had always been a bad sitter.

THE TALE OF
SAMUEL
WHISKERS

Once upon a time there was an old cat, called Mrs Tabitha Twitchit,
who was an anxious parent. She used to lose her kittens continually,
and whenever they were lost they were always in mischief!

On baking day Mrs Tabitha Twitchit determined to shut her kittens in a cupboard.

'And there you stay my two young rascals, until my baking is finished,' she said to Moppet and Mittens.

But she could not find Tom.

Tom Kitten did *not* want to be shut in a cupboard, so he looked around for a convenient place to hide and fixed upon the chimney.

Inside the chimney, Tom coughed and choked with the smoke. He began to climb right to the top.

'I cannot go back. If I slipped I might fall in the fire and singe my beautiful tail and my little blue jacket,' he said.

While Mrs Tabitha Twitchit was searching for Tom, Moppet and Mittens pushed open the cupboard door. They went straight to the dough which was set to rise in a pan in front of the fire.

'Shall we make dear little muffins?' said Mittens to Moppet.

But just at that moment, somebody knocked at the door, and a voice called out: 'Tabitha! Are you at home, Tabitha?'

'Oh, come in Cousin Ribby. I'm in sad trouble. I've lost my dear son Thomas. I'm afraid the rats have got him,' sobbed Mrs Tabitha Twitchit. 'And now Moppet and Mittens are gone too. What it is to have an unruly family,' she wailed.

'Well Cousin, we shan't find any of them standing here,' said Ribby firmly. 'I'm not afraid of rats. I'll help you find Tom - and whip him too. Now, just where would a naughty kitten hide?'

Meanwhile, up the chimney Tom Kitten was getting very frightened! It was confusing in the dark, and he felt quite lost.

All at once he fell head over heels down a hole and landed on a heap of very dirty rags.

'What a peculiar smell,' said Tom Kitten to himself. 'It's something like a mouse . . . only dreadfully strong . . . Oh!' he gasped suddenly.

Opposite to him - as far away as he could sit - was an enormous rat.

'What do you mean by tumbling into my bed all covered with smuts?' asked the rat (whose name was Samuel Whiskers).

'Please sir, the chimney wants sweeping,' said poor Tom Kitten miserably.

'Anna Maria! Anna Maria!' Samuel Whiskers called.
  There was a pattering noise and an old woman rat poked her head round a rafter.

'What have we here, Samuel?' she asked. 'A tasty morsel indeed!' She rushed upon Tom and before he knew what was happening, he was rolled up in a bundle, and tied with string in very tight knots.

'Anna Maria,' said the old man rat,
'make me a kitten dumpling
roly-poly pudding for my dinner.'

'Hmm . . . it requires dough and a pat of butter and a rolling-pin,'
said Anna Maria.
  The two rats consulted together for a few minutes and then went away.

Samuel Whiskers went boldly down the front staircase to the dairy to get the butter.

He made a second journey for the rolling-pin, which he pushed in front of him with his paws.

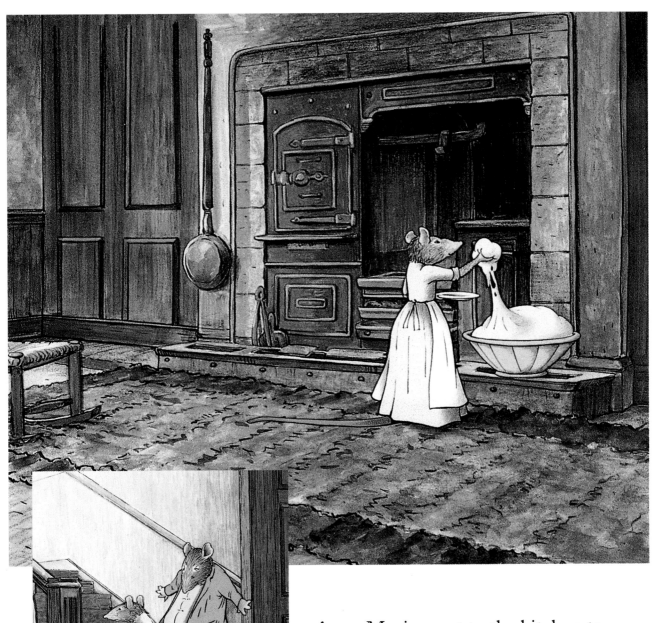

Anna Maria went to the kitchen to
steal the dough. She borrowed a
small saucer, and scooped up the
dough with her paws.

 'He is rather a large kitten for his
age,' she muttered, as she scooped
up another pawful.

Presently the rats came back and set to work to make Tom Kitten into a dumpling. First they smeared him with butter, and then they rolled him in the dough.

Ribby and Mrs Tabitha Twitchit heard a curious roly-poly noise under the attic floor, but there was nothing to be seen so they returned to the kitchen. Ribby found Moppet hiding in a flour barrel.

'Moppet!' scolded Mrs Twitchit.

'But mother,' cried Moppet, 'there's been an old woman rat in the kitchen and she's stolen some of the dough!'

Mittens was found in the dairy,
hiding in an empty jar.

'There's been an old man rat in
the dairy, mother. He's stolen a pat
of butter and a rolling-pin!' Mittens
cried.

'Oh my poor son, Thomas!'
exclaimed Tabitha, wringing her
paws.

Ribby and Mrs Tabitha Twitchit rushed upstairs. Sure enough, the roly-poly noise was still going on quite distinctly under the attic floor.

  'Oh my goodness, this is serious, Cousin Tabitha,' said Ribby. 'We must send for John Joiner at once, with a saw.'

And what was happening to Tom Kitten? All this time, the two rats had been hard at work.

'Will not the string be very indigestible, Anna Maria?' inquired Samuel Whiskers.

'No, no, no. It is of no consequence,' she replied before turning to Tom. 'I do wish you would stop moving your head about. It disarranges the dough so.'

'Oh, Mr Joiner, this way,' said Cousin Ribby. 'We can hear the strangest sounds . . . I dread to think! Come along, follow me quickly now.'

'I do *not* think it will be a good pudding,' said Samuel Whiskers, looking at Tom Kitten. 'It smells sooty.'

Anna Maria was about to argue the point, when they heard noises up above - the rasping of a saw, and the noise of a little dog, scratching and yelping!

'We are discovered and interrupted, Anna Maria. Let us collect our property (and other people's) and depart at once. I fear that we shall be obliged to leave this pudding, but I am persuaded that the knots would have proved indigestible,' said Samuel Whiskers.

So it happened that by the time John Joiner had got the plank up there was nobody under the floor except the rolling-pin and Tom Kitten in a very dirty dumpling!

Samuel Whiskers and Anna Maria found a wheelbarrow belonging to Miss Potter which they borrowed and hastily filled with a quantity of bundles.

'There may just have been room for the pudding,' said Samuel Whiskers wistfully.

'I notice that *you* are not pushing the barrow,' retorted Anna Maria. 'You might be of another opinion if you were!'

Then Samuel Whiskers and Anna Maria made their way to Farmer Potatoes' hay barn and hauled their parcels with a bit of string to the top of the hay mow.

'Be quick,' urged Anna Maria, 'and tie the bundles on, or Miss Potter will be missing the barrow.'

The cat family quickly recovered. The dumpling was peeled off Tom Kitten and made separately into a pudding, with currants in it to hide the smuts. They had to put Tom Kitten into a hot bath to get the butter off.

  And after that, there were no more rats for a long time at Mrs Tabitha Twitchit's.

THE TALE OF
TWO BAD MICE
AND
JOHNNY TOWN-MOUSE

Once upon a time there was a very beautiful doll's-house; it was red brick with white windows, and it had a front door and a chimney.

It belonged to two dolls called Lucinda and Jane. Jane was the cook; but she never did any cooking, because the dinner had been bought ready-made, in a box full of shavings.

One morning Lucinda and Jane went out for a drive in the doll's perambulator. There was no one in the nursery and it was very quiet.

Presently, there was a little scratching noise in the corner where there was a mouse-hole under the skirting-board. Tom Thumb put out his head. A minute afterwards, Hunca Munca, his wife, put her head out too.

When they saw that there was no one in the nursery, they went cautiously across the hearthrug.

Hunca Munca pushed the front door — it was not locked. "Let's have a look inside" she said.

Tom Thumb and Hunca Munca went upstairs and peeped into the dining-room. Such a lovely dinner was laid out upon the table! There were tin spoons, and lead knives and forks, and two dolly-chairs. "All ready for us!" said Tom Thumb.

Tom Thumb set to work at once to carve the ham, but the knife crumpled up and hurt him; he put his finger in his mouth. "It's not cooked enough. It's hard. You have a try Hunca Munca."

  Hunca Munca stood up in her chair, and chopped at the ham with another lead knife. The ham broke off the plate with a jerk, and rolled under the table.

  "Let it alone," said Tom Thumb; "give me some fish, Hunca Munca!"

Hunca Munca tried every tin spoon in turn; the fish was glued to the dish.

Then Tom Thumb lost his temper. He put the ham in the middle of the floor, and hit it with the tongs and with the shovel — bang, bang, smash, smash! The ham flew all into pieces. Underneath the shiny paint it was made of nothing but plaster!

"It's no good. You can't eat it!" said Hunca Munca.

Then there was no end to the rage and disappointment of Tom Thumb and Hunca Munca. They broke up the pudding, the lobsters, the pears and the oranges. As the fish would not come off the plate, they put it into the red-hot crinkly paper fire in the kitchen; but it would not burn either.

Tom Thumb went up the chimney and looked out at the top — there was no soot. Hunca Munca found some tiny cans upon the dresser, labelled Rice, Coffee, Sago, but there was nothing inside except red and blue beads.

Then the mice went into the dolls' bedroom. Tom threw Jane's clothes out of the window. Hunca Munca bounced on the bed. After pulling half the feathers out of Lucinda's bolster, she remembered that she herself needed a feather bed. "Let's take this bolster back to our place," she said.

They carried the bolster
downstairs and across the
hearthrug. "I hope this
will be worth all this
work," said Tom Thumb.
It was difficult to squeeze
the bolster into the
mouse-hole, but they
managed it somehow.

"There. That's lovely!"
said Hunca Munca. "Now
let's go back and see what
else will be useful."

They went back and fetched a chair, a book-case, a bird-cage, and several small odds and ends. The book-case and the bird-cage would not go into the mouse-hole. Hunca Munca left them behind the coal-box, and went to fetch a cradle. "This will be fine for my babies," she said.

Hunca Munca was just returning with another chair, when suddenly there was a noise of talking outside upon the landing. The mice rushed back to their hole, and the dolls came into the nursery.

What a sight met the eyes of Jane and Lucinda!

"What has happened?" asked the little girl who owned the dolls-house.

"It must be mice!" said the nurse.

The book-case and the bird-cage were rescued from under the coal-box — but Hunca Munca has got the cradle, and some of Lucinda's clothes.

She also has some useful pots and pans, and several other things.

The little girl said, "I will get a policeman doll!"

But the nurse said, "I will set a mouse-trap!"

Hunca Munca and Tom Thumb were not the only mice causing trouble that day.

When the cook opened the vegetable hamper, out sprang a terrified Timmy Willie.

"A mouse! A mouse! Call the cat!" screamed the cook.

But Timmy Willie did not wait for the cat. He rushed along the skirting-board till he came to a little hole, and in he popped.

He dropped half a foot, and crashed into the
middle of a mouse dinner-party, breaking
three glasses.

"Who in the world is this?" inquired Johnny
Town-mouse. But after the first exclamation
of surprise, he instantly recovered his manners.

He introduced Timmy to nine other mice, all with long tails and white neck-ties. The dinner was of eight courses; not much of anything, but truly elegant. Timmy was very anxious to behave with good manners, but the continual noise upstairs made him so nervous that he dropped a plate.

"Never mind, they don't belong to us," said Johnny. "How did you come here?" he asked.

"I'm from the country," said Timmy Willie. He explained how he had seen the hamper by the garden gate and climbed in. After eating some peas, he had fallen fast asleep. He awoke in a fright, while the vegetable hamper was lifted into the carrier's cart. Then there was a jolting and a clattering of horses' feet. Timmy Willie trembled amongst the jumbled up vegetables.

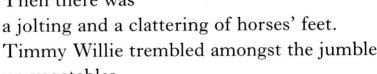
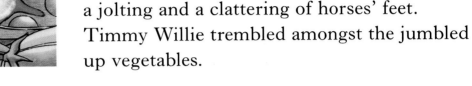

At last the cart stopped at a house and the hamper was carried in and set down.

The cook lifted the hamper lid and screamed at the sight of poor Timmy Willie.

"Then I fell in here," finished Timmy.

"And you are most welcome," said Johnny Town-mouse.

111

Timmy Willie felt quite faint. "Would you like to go to bed?" said Johnny. "I will show you a most comfortable sofa pillow".

"It is the best bed and I keep it exclusively for visitors," said Johnny Town-mouse. But the sofa smelt of cat. Timmy Willie preferred to spend a miserable night under the fender.

"Oh dear, oh dear!" he sighed. "I wish I was home."

The next day things were no better for Timmy Willie. He could not eat the food, and the noise prevented him from sleeping. In a few days he grew so thin that Johnny Town-mouse questioned him. "Are you ill?"

"Oh no," replied Timmy, "but I do so miss my peaceful sunny bank and my friend, Cock Robin."

"Well," said Johnny Town-mouse, "it may be that your teeth and digestion are unaccustomed to our food. Perhaps it might be wiser for you to return the way you came — in the hamper, to your own home in the country."

"Oh? Oh!" cried Timmy.

"Why of course. Did you not know that the hamper goes back empty on Saturdays?" said Johnny, rather huffily.

So Timmy Willie said goodbye to his new friends and hid in the hamper with a crumb of cake.

After much jolting, he was set down safely in his own garden.

"How good to be back!" said Timmy, in delight.

Sometimes on Saturdays he went to look at the hamper lying by the gate, but he knew better than to get in again. And nobody got out, though Johnny Town-mouse had half promised a visit.

*

Timmy Willie slept through the winter and the sun came out again in Spring.

Timmy Willie had nearly forgotten his visit to the town, when up the sandy path all spick and span with a brown leather bag came Johnny Town-mouse!

Timmy Willie received him with open arms. "You have come at the best of times. We will have herb pudding and sit in the sun."

"Hmm! It is a little damp" said Johnny Town-mouse.

"How are Tom Thumb and all our friends?" asked Timmy.

Johnny explained that the family had gone to the seaside. The cook was doing spring cleaning, with particular instructions to clear out the mice. There were four kittens and the cat had killed the canary.

"Tom Thumb has told the small mice all about the trap, and Hunca Munca has become quite good friends with the policeman-doll, although he never says anything, and always looks quite stern," said Johnny.

"What is that fearful noise?" asked Johnny Town-mouse.

"Oh, that's only a cow." said Timmy. "I will go and beg a little milk."

They were just setting off down the path, when Cock Robin flew down.

"Hide!" shouted Johnny, in fright.

"It's only my friend Cock Robin saying hello. Come along, Johnny, we haven't got all day."

"Whatever is that fearful racket?" said Johnny Town-mouse.

"That's only the lawn-mower," said Timmy. "Now we can fetch some fresh grass clippings to make up your bed."

Johnny waited while Timmy went to fetch the milk and the fresh grass. When he returned, it began to rain. "Oh! My tail is getting all wet!" complained Johnny.

"It's only a spring shower. Here, take this leaf and hold it over your head like this," said Timmy. "The rain will brighten up the flowers. Come along, Johnny."

"I am sure you will never want to live in town again," said Timmy Willie to Johnny Town-mouse.

But he did! He went back in the very next hamper of vegetables. He said it was too quiet.

Johnny got back safely to his town-house and his old friends.

As for the two bad mice, they were not so very naughty after all, because Tom Thumb paid for everything he broke. He found a crooked sixpence under the hearthrug; and upon Christmas Eve, he and Hunca Munca stuffed it into one of the stockings of Lucinda and Jane.

  And very early every morning, Hunca Munca comes with her dustpan and broom to sweep the dollies' house!

But Timmy Willie stayed in the country and he never went to town again. One place suits one person, another place suits another person. For my part I prefer to live in the country, like Timmy Willie.